Toby and the Mysterious Creature

Jean Lemieux

Illustrations by Sophie Casson
Translated by Sarah Cummins

Formac Publishing Company Limited
Halifax

Originally published as *Le chasseur de pistou*
Copyright © 2007 Les éditions de la courte échelle inc.
Translation copyright © 2008 Sarah Cummins

Formac Publishing Company Limited acknowledges the support of the
Cultural Affairs Section, Nova Scotia Department of Tourism, Culture
and Heritage. We acknowledge the financial support of the
Government of Canada through the Book Publishing Industry
Development Program (BPIDP) for our publishing activities.

We acknowledge the support of the Canada Council for the Arts for
our publishing program.

NOVA SCOTIA
Tourism, Culture and Heritage

The Canada Council | Le Conseil des Arts
for the Arts | du Canada

Library and Archives Canada Cataloguing in Publication

Lemieux, Jean, 1954-
[Chasseur de pistou. English]
    Toby and the mysterious creature / Jean Lemieux ; illustrated by
Sophie Casson; translated by Sarah Cummins.

(First novels)
Translation of: Le chasseur de pistou.
ISBN 978-0-88780-761-9 (bound).—ISBN 978-0-88780-759-6 (pbk.)

    I. Casson, Sophie II. Cummins, Sarah III. Title : Chasseur de
pistou. English. IV. Series.

PS8573.E5427C5213 2008   jC843'.54   C2008-904176-32

Formac Publishing Company Limited
5502 Atlantic Street
Halifax, NS B3H 1G4
www.formac.ca

Printed and bound in Canada

Distributed in the
United States by:
Orca Book Publishers
P.O. Box 468
Custer, WA U.S.A.
98240-0468

Table of Contents

To my sister Madeleine, the pistou expert

1

The Big Day

The big day had finally come.

It was June. In less than a week, summer vacation would begin. My friend Marianne and I were walking to school together.

We've known each other since kindergarten. We make a fantastic team. There's me — Toby Omeranovic, weighing in at twenty-five kilos, the heavyweight champion of questions. And there's Marianne, the champion of answers.

We were feeling good. The weather was fine, without a cloud in the sky. Sparrows chirped in the trees and on the clothes-lines.

I should have been content to just bask in the sunshine and listen to the birds chirping. But no! Something was bothering me.

"Marianne, do you think we're

prepared?"

"Of course we're prepared. We ran though it twice yesterday for your parents."

"I get nervous speaking in front of the class. I have to remember not to get the Sun and the Moon mixed up."

"Don't worry. Everything will be fine. You know all about eclipses, inside and out."

Sometimes I think the reason Marianne is the champion of answers is because she doesn't ask too many questions.

★ ★ ★

The big day was the last day of the contest.

Our teacher, Mrs. Dasgupta, had decided to hold a contest for the last presentation of the year. The prize was two tickets to go with her to see the Star Circus. The contest rules were simple. You had to bring something original to class and talk about it for ten minutes.

So far we had heard about a lot of things: a ukulele, a Swiss Army knife with twenty-one accessories, a collection of old-fashioned wooden toys, a pair of old rawhide snowshoes, and an Arab cloak called a burnoose, with matching turban, for example.

Liam and Michael, my sworn enemies, had tried to impress the class by bringing in a weasel.

The Liamichaels (that's what we call them) were not a hit. First of all, Mrs. Dasgupta is afraid of little animals. Plus

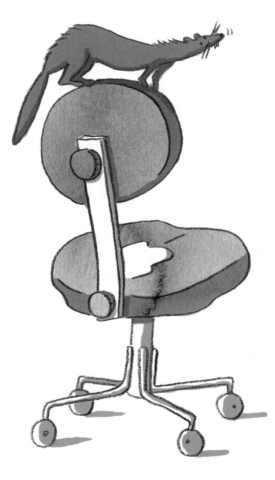

they made a few mistakes in their presentation. And some of the kids said that animals were not objects.

The class voted on this question. It was decided by only two votes that animals could be considered objects, at least until the contest was over. Unfortunately for the Liamichaels, the weasel peed on Mrs. Dasgupta's chair. I thought they were out of the running.

Marianne and I figured we had a good chance to win, because we had put together a fantastic presentation.

What's more, after us there was only one other team left, and it wasn't even a team. It was Merlin Higginbottom-Campari all by himself. He is so shy that we wondered if he could last ten minutes.

Marianne and I entered the schoolyard, our hearts beating fast.

2

A Trip Around the Sky

After math class, it was time for the presentations.

Marianne and I stood in front of the blackboard. Sweat was trickling down my back. Although the windows were open, it was hot in the classroom.

On Mrs. Dasgupta's desk I placed a package, wrapped like a gift with bows of every colour.

"FELLOW STUDENTS!" I began.

Whoops! That was a bit too loud.

"Fellow students," I said again, in a quieter voice.

Marianne took her mother's alarm clock out of a bag. It had enormous steel bells on top. When it rang, it was worse than the fire alarm.

"Today Marianne and I are going to tell you about a very interesting topic, so interesting that we need the alarm clock so we won't go over our ten minutes."

There were a few laughs ... it was better than nothing.

"We have brought in something that is normally ten thousand million times bigger than the classroom. We refer, of course, to —"

"TA-DUM!" said Marianne.

"THE MOON!"

I pulled an exact replica of the Moon from the bag. There was no reaction from the class. From far off, it must have looked like a marbly bowling ball.

"This mini-moon is not just any mini-moon! My father brought it back from a trip to NASA in the United States. NASA is where the Americans launch rockets and satellites and space sputtles."

"Space SHUTTLES," Marianne corrected me.

"Yes, the space shuttles that you see on television. On this reproduction you can see all the features of the moon in person!"

Then Marianne told the class all about

lunar geography. The moon has two sides — the visible side and the hidden, dark side. There are seas with no water. They have funny names like the Sea of Serenity and the Sea of Tranquillity.

"But we didn't just bring the moon," Marianne went on. "We brought the Earth as well!"

I pulled out a soccer ball with the word 'Earth' written on it in marker.

"And the sun too!"

And I took out a flashlight that I had wrapped up in papier-mâché, painted bright red. This time the whole class laughed. I had no idea why.

"And now we're going to tell you all about ECLIPSES!"

I turned on the flashlight and Marianne

held the moon and the earth, one in each hand. I was the sun.

We rotated around the classroom, explaining what happens when there is a lunar eclipse and a solar eclipse. It's not

that complicated. An eclipse happens when the three heavenly bodies are aligned.

DRINGGG!!!

The alarm clock went off at just the right time.

"Next time we'll bring in something even more original," I said to finish.

Everyone listened quietly to hear what that could be.

"A weasel that doesn't pee!"

I don't know what came over me. That wasn't part of the presentation. Even so, everyone laughed their heads off. Even Mrs. Dasgupta, and she doesn't laugh that easily.

Well, actually, not everyone laughed. The Liamichaels didn't think it was funny at all.

3

Merlin Higginbottom-Campari

Marianne and I went back to our seats and Merlin Higginbottom-Campari, the last contestant, went and stood behind Mrs. Dasgupta's desk. In his hand he held a square green box, hardly big enough to hold a tennis ball.

Before I go on, I should tell you about Merlin Higginbottom-Campari.

First of all, he's a new kid in our school. He came to our class two months ago. When Mrs. Dasgupta introduced him, she said that Merlin came from Ivory Coast, in Africa.

That surprised us. Merlin doesn't look like an African, because he isn't black-skinned. There are several African kids at the school, from Senegal and Rwanda and Congo. They all have black skin.

But Merlin is different. His skin isn't white like most of the other kids is. Nor is it yellow or black. In fact, Merlin is a strange colour, a kind of pale green or dark beige.

He speaks with an accent and uses words

that sound like they come from a book.

One day, when we were playing ball in the park, I asked him what nationality he was. By using the word 'nationality', I wanted to show him that I could read books too.

"I don't know," he replied. "My mother is French. At least, I think she is."

"What about your father?"

"He's a mixture."

A mixture? Is there such a thing as a mixed nationality?

Merlin told me that his dad was born in Portugal, but his family came from Egypt, Greece, Italy and Brazil. Just to make things simpler, Merlin himself had lived in France, Malaysia, Chile, and finally, Ivory Coast.

In other words, Merlin Higginbottom-Campari is a walking atlas. No wonder he's pale green. He must have gotten seasick from travelling all over the globe.

I have always lived in the same house in the same town. I envied Merlin a little bit. I asked him what his father did.

"He's a wind scientist."

"What about your mother?"

"She plays the piano."

"Is that all she does?"

"No. At night, she sleeps."

So, Merlin Higginbottom-Campari came from a wind specialist and a piano player.

He is the shortest kid in the class. He is as skinny as a tree in winter. Merlin is always listening to music. One day Mrs.

Dasgupta had to confiscate his player because he was listening to it in class.

She could have just let him listen. He never needs to pay attention to what the teacher says, because he already has everything in his head.

I thought I knew a lot of things for an eight-year-old, but Merlin is way ahead of me. He doesn't show off, though. He hardly ever talks to the other kids. He just stays in his corner and doesn't mix in.

There were now twenty-three kids in the class, and I always thought of Merlin as the twenty-third. Not just because he was the last one to join the class. It's just that he always seems to be different from the rest of the kids.

I don't know why Mrs. Dasgupta didn't

make him join a team of two persons. She usually tries to make us work in teams.

I watched Merlin standing alone in front of the class. He gently set his little green box on Mrs. Dasgupta's desk. He was pale and his hand was shaking. I winked at

Marianne. We were sure to win the tickets to the circus!

And then Merlin started telling us about the pistou.

4

One Strange Animal

The class was restless. Mrs. Dasgupta was about to say "Now, children!" the way she always does, but Merlin Higginbottom-Campari beat her to it.

"Now, children!" he said, imitating her tone of voice and accent perfectly. Everyone started laughing.

We looked at Mrs. Dasgupta. She

seemed to think it was pretty funny too. I don't know how he does it, but the walking atlas has got her wrapped around his little finger.

"Today, I am going to tell you about the pistou," said Merlin. "Does anybody know about the kind of pistou that is used in cooking?"

Only one person raised his hand — Sonny Chiodini. He's Italian.

"Well, I know about pesto," he said.

"Ah!" cried Merlin. "Pistou is the French version of pesto, a mixture of garlic, basil, olive oil and pine nuts."

"YUCK!" said Sigi.

"Don't worry," said Merlin, holding up his hands. "I'm not going to talk about that kind of pistou. What I brought in today is the other kind of pistou."

He widened his eyes and rolled them from side to side, as if he had brought in an Egyptian mummy or King Kong. He is not only a talking book — Merlin is quite a talented performer too!

"First of all, the pistou is an animal. What kind of animal? Some say it is a bird. Others claim it is a fish. But scientists in

New Zealand have declared that the pistou is descended from a small snake called Crotalus putt-puttis.

"Where does the pistou live? Everywhere and nowhere. The pistou is very difficult to observe and to capture. A sect in Arizona maintains that the pistou is a miniature extraterrestrial. It has been spotted in Indonesia, Russia and Tickle Cove."

The class was as quiet as a cemetery. Everyone was hanging on Merlin's words. Finally, my friend Catherine Bainbridge-Babcock, known as Beebee, could contain her curiosity no longer. She raised her hand.

"Do you have a real pistou in that box?"

"Of course."

"How did you catch it?"

"It was very, very difficult. The pistou hunts at the break of day. The rest of the time it spends sleeping, hidden away inside a flower. In fact, the pistou may be a kind of prehistoric bumblebee. It's really a very strange animal. You can only catch it in a dream."

"In a dream?" Sigi asked skeptically.

"It can only be captured by a sleepwalker. I caught this pistou last night in our backyard. I was walking like this ..."

Merlin held his arms out, closed his eyes, and began to stagger around recklessly among the desks.

"Finally, I came to a large tulip. I began to whistle 'Twinkle, twinkle, little star', and the pistou came out of its flower. I coaxed

it onto my shoulder and brought it back to my bedroom."

"Why did you whistle 'Twinkle, twinkle, little star'?"

"All the books on pistouology say to do that. The pistou becomes totally helpless when it hears 'Twinkle, twinkle, little star'."

I was beginning to think Merlin was making some of this up.

"Just like a chameleon," he went on, "the pistou can disguise itself by taking on the colouring of its surroundings. When it flies, it takes on the colour of the air!" That was enough for me. I raised my hand.

"We want to SEE this pistou!" I demanded.

All the kids agreed. They began to chant: "WE want to SEE! WE want to SEE!"

"All right," said Merlin.

He bent over the little green box. The class fell silent. Carefully, cautiously, he lifted up the lid and —

BZZZZZZZZZ!

Merlin tried to catch the pistou in his hands, but it escaped. He waved his arms around and ran through the classroom, calling, "There it is! There it is! Catch it!"

I didn't see anything. I thought it was Merlin making the buzzing sound as he ran around the room. The class was in an uproar. Everyone was yelling, "I see it!" but nobody really saw anything.

Finally, Merlin climbed onto a desk and then onto the windowsill, flapping his hands. The buzzing stopped. He turned back to the class.

"The pistou has escaped out the window," he announced. "How unfortunate."

Judging from the smile on his face, he was not sorry at all. He returned to his

place at the front of the class and made a little bow.

"That's the end of my presentation."

No one was listening to him. Everyone

had rushed to the window, hoping to see the famous fleeing pistou.

Mrs. Dasgupta had not moved from her chair.

"Now, children!" she said sharply, and began to clap her hands for Merlin, all by herself. The kids went back to their seats and started to applaud too. Some of them even whistled and banged on their desks!

Marianne and I looked at one another. We might as well forget about the circus.

5

Cheats and Dirty Tricks

At recess, Marianne, Beebee and I met up under our favourite tree. I was so mad I was red in the face.

"Merlin cheated! There's no such thing as a pistou!"

"But I saw it! I swear!" insisted Beebee.

Of all our friends, Beebee is the most gullible. Once I made her believe my grandfather was a cousin of Santa Claus.

"I checked in the dictionary," I said. "There is no animal called a pistou. Merlin brought NOTHING to school. He did a presentation on NOTHING!"

"Can nothing be considered to be an object?" Marianne wondered.

But we had no time to debate the question, as Beebee cried, "Watch out, Toby! Here come the Liamichaels!"

I turned around. Liam and Michael were heading towards us. In fact, from the way they stared, I could tell they were heading for me. And they were not in a good mood.

The problem with the Liamichaels is that they are big and strong and kind of mean. There was no point in running away.

They could run faster than me, and I would look like a scaredy-cat.

Liam was hiding something in his hand. I turned to face them.

"What is it?"

Michael grabbed me by the collar and hauled me up like a sack of potatoes.

"Let him go!" cried Marianne.

"I'm going to tell Mrs. Dasgupta!" Beebee threatened, trembling like a leaf.

Michael looked at them scornfully and said, "Keep quiet, you pipsqueaks, if you know what's good for you."

Then he turned to me. "So you laughed at our weasel, Toby?"

"Now YOU get to pee!" sneered Liam.

Before I could do anything, Liam yanked at my belt and poured a bottle of

sparkling water down my underpants! Let me tell you, that does not feel good.

"That's for starters," said Michael. "We'll be waiting for you after school."

He let go of me and the Liamichaels walked off, pleased with themselves. My pants were all wet. I could feel the water trickling down my legs and into my shoes.

Here it was, the big day of the contest, and I, Toby Omeranovic, looked like a baby who had peed his pants!

What was worse, the Liamichaels would be waiting for me after school! Usually when they wait for someone after school, it's not to wish them a pleasant evening.

What should I do? Marianne and Beebee tried to comfort me, but I could tell they wanted to laugh. They hate the

Liamichaels too, but they still thought I was pretty funny in my wet pants!

The bell rang for the end of recess. There was no way I was going back in to face the class.

Without a word to anyone, I left the schoolyard. I ran and ran all the way home. I knew it wasn't allowed, but I couldn't help it.

6

Consequences

Back home, I went inside, got undressed, washed off, and put on fresh clothes — all in record time.

The schoolyard was deserted when I got back. I slipped through the cloakroom and down the hall. Still nobody.

With a heavy heart, I gently opened the door to the classroom and peeked in. Mrs.

Dasgupta was at the blackboard and she pretended not to see me. What a terrible way to end the school year!

I went to my seat. I felt angry and sad. My big day had turned into a puny day.

The Liamichaels looked at me and smirked. What were they cooking up?

I was so upset that I didn't even notice Mrs. Dasgupta was announcing the contest winners.

"In second place, Marianne Landry and Toby Omeranovic!"

The class applauded, but it didn't make me feel any better. Second place or last place, it was all the same to me.

"And in first place," Mrs. Dasgupta went on, "Merlin Higginbottom-Campari, for his presentation on the pistou!"

The worst of it all is that Merlin didn't even look happy! He accepted his ticket to the circus in silence, without even a smile, as if it were a punishment.

That made me even madder. Merlin presents an animal that doesn't even exist, and he wins the contest!

Sonny Chiodini raised his hand.

"There were two prize tickets. Merlin gave his presentation alone. So who gets to go to the circus with you and Merlin?"

Mrs. Dasgupta smiled.

"I managed to get another ticket. So I will be going to the circus with Merlin, Marianne, and ..."

She paused and shot me a strange look.

"Even though I am not sure he deserves it, I also plan to take Toby."

7

The Hidden Side of Merlin

I was glad I was going to go to the circus, but I felt uneasy. The threat from the Liamichaels hung over me. When Mrs. Dasgupta turned her back, Michael shook his fist at me and Liam drew his finger across his throat.

It was not a good sign.

During the afternoon recess I went and

hid in the washroom. I tried to think of a way to avoid the Liamichaels. Maybe I

could sneak onto the school bus and have it drop me off near my house?

Then I had a better idea. When we went back into class, I crossed my arms on the desk and lay my head on them. Mrs. Dasgupta soon noticed.

"What's the matter, Toby?"

"I'm SIIIICK. I feel like I'm going to throw up."

"You are no more sick than I am," said Mrs. Dasgupta firmly. "Get back to work. Now."

She seemed so sure of herself that I obeyed. How did she know I was only pretending to be sick?

Time ticked on. In only half an hour, the bell would ring. I had a knot in my stomach that felt as big as the moon. If it got any worse, I wouldn't have to pretend to be sick.

I watched the Liamichaels out of the corner of my eye. They were quiet now. They must have had their plan all set.

There was only one escape. I had to leave before they did and run home as fast as I could. So what if the other kids thought I was chicken? At least I would be safe.

I put my books and pencil case into my backpack and checked that my shoelaces were tied. I was ready to take off.

The Liamichaels hadn't gotten anything ready. They weren't even looking at me anymore. I don't know what it was, but they didn't seem well.

DRING! There was the bell! I was off

like a sprinter when Mrs. Dasgupta's voice rang out too.

"Toby! I need to speak to you."

Bad luck! My chest felt tight as I returned to my seat. One by one the other kids left the classroom. The Liamichaels left too, without a threat, without even looking in my direction.

I was alone with Mrs. Dasgupta. She put her books away and then sat down at her desk. The whole school was quiet now. She looked at me sternly.

"Toby, I am not very proud of you."

I didn't answer. I was thinking about the Liamichaels. They were probably waiting for me in the schoolyard. Now there was no chance of escape.

"First of all, you made fun of Liam and

Michael's presentation, in front of the whole class. I know they aren't always kind to you either, but …"

"What do you mean, they're not always kind to me? They deliberately soaked my pants!"

Mrs. Dasgupta motioned for me to be quiet.

"I know what happened. Liam and Michael have their faults. But you won't make them behave better by making fun of them."

Now Mrs. Dasgupta was defending the Liamichaels! What next?

"Secondly," she went on, "you left the school without asking permission. You know that is not allowed. Tomorrow, you will have a detention and you will help me clean the classroom. Do you understand?"

I nodded. Hope was returning. If Mrs. Dasgupta kept me late enough, the Liamichaels might get tired of waiting and would go home.

"The third thing is more serious. You weren't happy that Merlin won the contest, were you?"

I felt redness rise in my face, like when you put a thermometer onto a space heater.

"Uh … it wasn't fair. He gave a presentation on a pistou that doesn't even exist!"

"Are you a bit jealous of him perhaps?"

Jealous? Me, Toby Omeranovic, jealous of Merlin Higginbottom-Campari? I wanted to deny it, but I knew Mrs. Dasgupta might be right.

"Maybe …"

Whew! All of a sudden I felt much better. Yes, it was true. I was jealous of Merlin Higginbottom-Campari. He is very smart. He's been all over the world. He talks like a book.

I didn't dare say it, but I had a feeling he had become the teacher's pet.

"Did you wonder why it was that Merlin did his presentation alone?"

"Nothing new about that. He's always alone."

"He's alone because he feels the class has never accepted him. He comes from a foreign country. It's not easy for him to fit in."

I didn't say anything. It was true I could have tried harder to be nice to Merlin. Mrs. Dasgupta looked at me with her sharp eyes that saw everything. Soon the school year would be over. She had been hard on me sometimes, but I would miss her.

"What's more," she went on, "I think that Merlin would like to be friends with you."

"Why do you think that?"

"You should be grateful to him. He told me what was going on with Liam and Michael. You can go home now. Nothing will happen to you."

I thanked Mrs. Dasgupta. When I went back to my desk, I saw that Marianne had forgotten the props we had used for our presentation.

I put the alarm clock, the moon, the earth and the sun in a plastic bag and slung it over my shoulder.

It was pretty heavy, along with my backpack stuffed with books. But I didn't mind! I had been saved from the Liamichaels, and I felt as light as a … pistou!

Someone was waiting for me in the schoolyard. It was Merlin, sitting under the basketball hoop. When I went over to him, he took off his earphones.

"I was watching out," he said. "In case those ruffians got it in their heads to set an ambush."

I told you he talks like a book! This time, I think he was doing it on purpose, to make a joke.

"Thanks."

I held out my hand. My bag of props fell on the ground. I hoped the flashlight hadn't broken.

"Would you like me to carry your planets?" offered Merlin.

I accepted his offer and asked if he would like to come have a snack at my house. He was happy, and so was I.

We set off together. It was still nice

outside. The birds were still singing in the trees and on the clothes-lines.

"Congratulations," I told Merlin, "That

pistou was a great invention."

"What do you mean, an invention? Every word I said was true!"

The worst of it was that he was serious. I have a feeling we'll be taking care of that pistou for most of the summer!

More novels in the *First Novels* series!

Raffi's Island Adventure
Sylvain Meunier
Illustrated by Élisabeth Eudes-Pascal

Raffi McCaffery is proud! He stands on a rock on an island, facing the sea. For him, this is a great victory, having had trouble walking for so long. For the first time, Raffi can go camping with his father and his friend Carlito. Two days without having to listen to his sister, what a vacation!

To make things even better, he can watch the puffins, grill hot dogs over the fire and explore a deserted island. But is the island really deserted? Soon the discoveries begin, and sleeping under the stars brings many surprises.

Pucker Up, Morgan
Ted Staunton
Illustrated by Bill Slavin

Morgan is delighted to have the lead role in *The Frog Prince* even if he has to kiss Aldeen, the Godzilla of Grade Three, to turn into a prince. They both agree smooching is gross. Despite Aldeen's threats and Morgan's overreacting they manage to create an unexpected twist to the play. Morgan discovers that teamwork makes a better performance.

Robyn's Monster Play

Hazel Hutchins

Illustrated by Yvonne Cathcart

Robyn feels *The Raft*, the class play, is unfair because it casts only three roles to the boys known as the 3G's. Robyn starts her own play, *The Monster that Ate the World*, and learns how difficult it is to organize everything by herself. With the help of some classmates Robyn pulls it off, and finds that her feelings change.